LADYBIRD BOOKS, INC.
Auburn, Maine 04210 U.S.A.

Printed in England (3)

BiG HUG
A Busy Day

By JOHN GRACE
Illustrated by STUART TROTTER

Ladybird Books

wet

dry

clean

push

up

down

lost

found

on

in

out

light

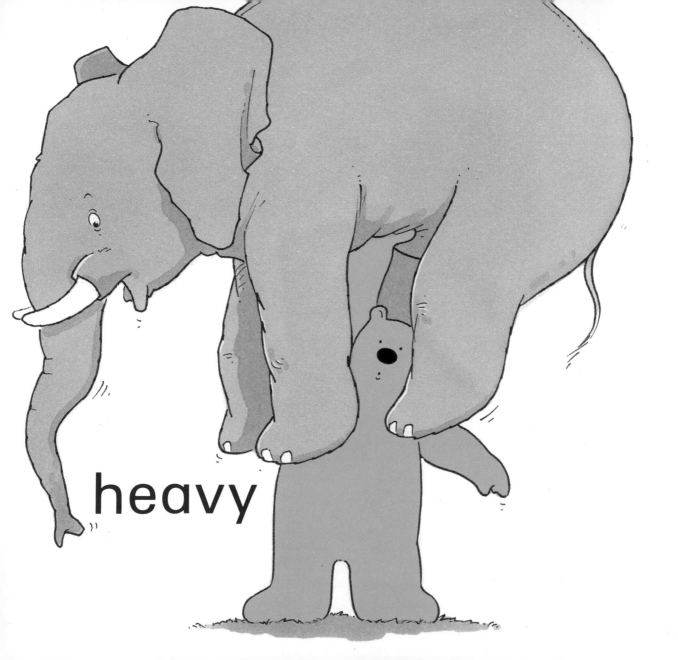

heavy

asleep

awake

fast

"What have you
been doing today?"
asked Yopple the turtle.

'Oh, nothing much," said Big Hug.